Day of

Herobrine's Quest – Book No. 3

by Steve DeWinter

Disclaimer:

Summary

Now inside the real world replica Minecraft program, Josh, Andre, and Suzy can only get out once they locate Herobrine. On their journey they decide to stop at a walled-in city to find information about which way Herobrine might be traveling, and discover the town is under siege by Creepers.

Do you want the author of this book to visit your classroom?

Ask your teacher to contact Steve DeWinter at writer@stevedw.com to discuss having an author visit with your class using the power of the internet and a webcam.

Watch Steve and his son, the real Josh who inspired the Josh in this story, play games and have fun together on their YouTube Channel.

https://www.youtube.com/c/odnttv

Ramblin' Prose Publishing

Copyright © 2015 Steve DeWinter

HEROBRINE'S QUEST is a trademark of Ramblin' Prose Publishing.

eBook Edition

ISBN-10: 1-61978-116-6

ISBN-13: 978-1-61978-116-0

Paperback Edition

ISBN-10: 1-61978-117-4

ISBN-13: 978-1-61978-117-7

Chapter 1

Mason edged his way along the stone wall of the underground tunnel. The farther he moved away from the torch behind him, the dimmer the tunnel ahead became.

As soon as he could no longer differentiate the shadows from the darkness, he pulled another torch from the pack on his back, lit it, and tucked it into a crevice in the wall. The sudden flare of light chased the shadows deeper into the tunnel ahead.

He continued slowly creeping down the tunnel, placing torches every thirty paces, until he reached his destination.

The tunnel opened into a wider

underground cavern. The light from the torch he had just placed barely cut into the overwhelming darkness of the open space. He reached into his pack for another torch, only to find it empty.

He had used all the torches to light the tunnels that led to this place. He had to go back and get more. He planned to probe deeper into the caverns to find the item that would free his town from the plague that kept them all living in fear.

At least the lit torches would lead him back out to the relative safety of the surface. He had started his journey as soon as daylight broke, so he would be able to make it out, and back home, safe inside the secure walls of Estermead, well before sunset.

He turned around and looked down the long tunnel at the receding dots of flickering light. He did a double take and silently counted the number of flaming torches.

There should be more.

Just then, the farthest torch flickered and went out. If he hadn't been looking right at it he might not have noticed.

He shivered as he realized that all the torches beyond that one were also dark. Without the torches leading the way, he might never find his way back out of the labyrinthine caves. The flame on the next farthest torch wavered, and went out.

He stood stock still as, one by one, the torches fluttered in response to some unseen breeze and winked out of existence.

He backed into the cavern as he watched all but the last torch go out. His heart thudded deep in his chest as he watched the flame on that last torch begin to dance wildly. Right before it went out, he saw the terrifying mottled green face, with the perpetual frown, lean in close to the flame and blow it out.

Darkness enveloped him leaving him blind. He would have to rely on his sense of hearing and touch to escape.

He slipped his bow from around his

shoulder, yanked an arrow from the quiver on his back, and notched it to the bowstring.

A Creeper had blown out the torch.

They had never done that before.

They were learning.

But who was teaching them?

He pulled back on the arrow, the bow bending tightly, and turned his head to listen for the faint sound of dry leaves blowing in the wind.

The sound pierced the darkness to his left. He adjusted his aim and let go of the arrow.

It whistled through the air and splintered when it collided with the stone wall of the cavern. He pulled the next arrow from his quiver, notched it, and drew back.

The same sound came at him from his right. He adjusted his aim and shot. The arrow flew into the distance, only to skip on the ground as it failed to find its target.

He felt behind him in the quiver.

One arrow left.

He notched it and pulled the bow tight, his muscles straining to hold it steady, and listened.

His skin crawled as an unnerving hiss echoed in the blackness behind him.

The same hiss that always preceded the explosion.

His sister's smiling face was the last thing

on his mind as he felt the concussive wave hit him.

Chapter 2

Josh folded the map and placed it into his bag with one hand while he steadied his horse with the other. "According to the map, the next town is Estermead."

Andre pulled hard to keep from being dragged across the ground by his horse. "Tell me again why we are walking?"

Suzy's horse walked alongside her and she barely had to keep hold of the reins. "We don't get tired, but they do."

Andre pulled harder to keep his horse on the road as it spotted a tasty bush and headed for it. "I know I wasn't the only one who heard Notch say we can fly here."

Josh steadied his horse and walked him around a gaping hole in the middle of the road. "He said to not let the people here see us fly."

Andre pulled his horse back onto the road. "Then we do it when nobody's looking."

Suzy patted her behaving horse. "It's too risky. We can't guarantee that no one would see us. I think it's safer to stay on the ground."

Andre steered his horse around another crater in the ground, but he was too close to the edge and the horse reared up, nearly knocking him into it. "Safer for whom?"

Josh looked at the craters ahead of them.

"We don't even know how to fly."

Andre stared at a farmhouse that was missing half of one wall, the floor dropping down into another crater. "I say we take the time to figure it out and not worry about what the neighbors will think."

Suzy stopped and pointed at the small village that looked like a war zone. "All of these houses have been blown up. What do you think did this?"

Josh stopped his horse before the edge of yet another massive crater in the road. "I've been noticing them too. They look abandoned. But if they were already empty, who would blow them up?"

Andre stopped next to Josh. "Creepers. I used to see this all the time in my villages when I'd spawn tons of them, set the mode to Survival, and try to see how long I could last. The end result usually looked a lot like this."

Suzy looked at the destruction all around them. "But Notch said this world was modeled after the real world. No Creepers, no Zombies, nothing like that."

Andre looked at her. "I guess someone has modded the program."

They all looked at each other and said simultaneously, "Herobrine."

A scream emanated from one of the burned out houses and they all turned toward it. A woman, wielding a pickaxe over her head, was running straight at them.

Suzy put her hands up and stepped toward the woman, who adjusted her direction, and ran straight at her, screaming a battle cry at the top of her lungs.

Suzy grabbed for the pickaxe as the woman swung it at her head.

The pickaxe sliced across Suzy's face and she stumbled backward and fell down.

Andre looked at the blood that streamed from the slice on her cheek. "He said we couldn't get hurt!"

The woman, satisfied she had already taken one of them down, turned her attention to

Andre, probably because he was the next closest to her. He backpedaled as she rushed at him.

"Whoa, whoa, whoa, whoa, whoa..." Andre yelled as he ducked under the swinging pickaxe. He turned and ran full speed across the field, hollering over his shoulder as he jumped the nearest fence. "Josh! Do something!"

Josh stepped into the middle of the road "Hey!"

The woman stopped her pursuit of Andre and spun around, the wild look in her eyes making him take a step backward. Whatever he had planned to do or say to her instantly melted away as she let out a blood curdling scream and charged at him.

Chapter 3

Josh kept backing up as the woman charged. As soon as she was close, she swung the pickaxe. He jumped forward, letting the handle catch him in the shoulder. The sudden jolt knocked the pickaxe out of the woman's hands, and it clattered to the ground.

Josh grabbed the woman and spun her around, holding her tightly from behind.

"Easy! It's okay, we're friends!"

She struggled against him, but he held her in an iron grip. "You said His name! Only those who do His bidding ever say His name!"

"Whose name?"

Andre ran up. "I'm guessing Herobrine?"

The woman began screaming again. Suzy stood up and stood in front of the woman who still struggled against Josh's grip. "We don't work for him."

The woman stopped struggling and looked at Suzy. "Then why dare speak His name?"

Suzy smiled back at her. "Because we're not afraid of him."

The woman's eyes suddenly grew larger and a look of panic spread across her face. "Your wound..."

Suzy touched her face and wiped away the blood. The cut had already sealed itself with a fresh scar.

The woman began struggling harder. "You're just like Him. Kill me quickly. Do not make me suffer."

Andre frowned. "We don't want to kill you."

The woman started crying and became dead weight as she stopped struggling and hung limply in Josh's arms. "Please. I beg of you. Do not make me suffer."

Josh lowered her gently to the ground. "We don't want to hurt you either."

She looked up at them. "So, you are not here because of Him?"

Andre bent down. "We came here looking for Him."

"To stop Him," Suzy added before the woman started crying again.

The woman wiped away her tears. "You're not here to kill us?"

Suzy placed a hand on her shoulder. "No. We're here to help."

The woman breathed a sigh of relief and smiled through the tears. "We knew someone would come to save us from the plague."

Suzy's forehead wrinkled. "What plague?"

"The Creepers. They come every night. We have been able to repair the damage they do, but their attacks are becoming more coordinated; less random. We can't keep up, so we sent messengers to the biggest cities asking for help. And now you have come."

Andre grabbed Suzy's arm and pulled her away out of earshot. Josh caught up with them just as Suzy pulled her arm out of his hand.

"Notch said not to interfere," Andre hissed loudly.

Suzy stared him down. "We're not. We're helping."

Andre looked at Josh. "We can't get involved in the problems of everyone we meet. We have to find..." He looked at the woman. "We have to find Him and go back home."

Suzy looked at the woman. "They have been dealing with Him for a hundred years.

Helping them is our best chance at finding Him."

Andre gave Josh a pleading look. "Tell Suzy we can't waste our time helping these people."

Josh stared at the woman. She smiled when their eyes met. He looked back at Andre. "She's right. They can help us find Him faster than we could on our own. If these people need someone to help them, then I guess we are the only ones around who can."

Andre grabbed him by the shoulders and shook him. "We're not heroes Josh."

Josh looked Andre in the eyes. "You're right." He looked over at Suzy, whose cut had healed completely as if it had never happened.

Not even a scar remained where the pickaxe had cut her.

"We're superheroes."

Chapter 4

The woman, she said her name was Elbertina, told them how her brother went missing after he volunteered to go into the Creeper caves to destroy their nest.

As she led them through the construction zone, the only opening in the city to the world outside its walls, she continued talking.

"After Mason disappeared a month ago, the Creepers came in greater numbers, all focusing their attacks on the same spot. Before then, it was random and we were able to deal with the damage as long as it was distributed all around the exterior wall. With them all attacking the same location, we can't rebuild it fast enough. If we don't stop them, the inner wall, and the city, will fall within the week."

Suzy gripped Elbertina's arm reassuringly. "We won't let that happen."

Elbertina smiled. "I'm so glad you answered our call for help."

Suzy smiled back. "So am I."

Elbertina led them to a ladder attached to the side of the inner wall. She pointed up. "Our best defense was to seal the city inside a wall without any gates or doors. By placing ladders at various points, we can still come and go as we please. Creepers have no arms, so they can't use the ladders."

As she climbed, she continued talking. "They got through the outer wall in the course of a week when they started concentrating their attacks on a single location. If it weren't for the archers, they would have overrun the inner wall and gotten into the city."

Suzy climbed after her. "When did the Creepers first start attacking?"

Elbertina clambered over the top of the wall and helped Suzy up. "They started long before I was born. It is said that only Sven the Elder knows why the Creepers came."

"They've been attacking your city every night all this time?"

"No. My parents said that they attacked the city for fifteen years until then one day, they just stopped. Within a few weeks with no sign of them, the elders began to venture out and build farms again. My parents were born during this time and it was thought that whatever had caused the Creepers in the first place was finally gone forever. And then five years ago, it started again without warning. Those who had gone to live outside the walls were attacked by the first wave of Creepers. Every night, more Creepers arrived to attack the city. Only, this time, for every one we killed, more came the next night."

Josh climbed over the edge and stood up.

"If Sven was the only one who knew why the Creepers attacked, did he know why they came back?"

Elbertina shook her head. "I asked my parents the same thing. Nobody asked him."

Andre hopped up to the top of the wall. "How come?"

"The last time someone tried, he bit them."

Andre frowned deeply. "Why would he do that?"

Elbertina sighed. "He went insane after the first Creeper attack. He's been locked up in the asylum ever since."

Chapter 5

They stood at the cave's entrance where Elbertina's brother had gone in, and never came back out, and watched as she rode one of their horses back to the safety of the city before the sun went down.

Upon hearing of the three brave heroes who were going to stop the Creepers, the townspeople had provided them with swords, bows and arrows, and torches. Everyone gave them pats on the back and offered a hearty "good luck" before quickly returning to work on the wall. There wasn't time to celebrate because nobody was willing to risk the safety of their city on strangers.

Even those claiming to not be afraid of Him.

It wasn't the first time someone arrived with a promise to rid the town of Creepers. And the town still had a major Creeper problem.

Once they could no longer see Elbertina in the distance, they turned back to the gaping mouth of the cave.

Andre let out a long breath. "Well, here we go."

Suzy brushed past him. "Quit being so dramatic."

She walked into the darkness of the cave

and faded from sight.

Her face lit up with the flare of her first torch as she used it to light another torch stuck on the wall. She looked back at the two boys. "Are you coming?"

Josh and Andre looked at each other and rushed in after her.

They traveled along the narrow tunnel, Suzy lighting torches already stuck in the wall as they moved forward. "These must be the torches Elbertina's brother used. But why are they still lit?"

Andre inspected one closely. "They didn't get used up. There's still plenty of charcloth wrapped around them. It's almost like someone blew them out."

Josh peered back, the trail of lit torches behind them showing the slight bend of the long tunnel they walked down. "I don't feel any wind down here, so that couldn't be it."

"Do you think whoever got to her brother down here put them out?" Andre said.

"We don't know what happened to her brother. For all we know, he could have gotten scared and left, too afraid to return to town as a failure."

Josh kept looking behind them as they walked when he noticed the farthest torch go out. He stopped and watched as the next one closer also went out. "Uh, guys?"

The other two stopped and looked at him. He pointed down the tunnel. "The torches are going out."

As all three of them looked down the tunnel in the direction Josh was pointing as the next torch flickered and went dark.

Chapter 6

One by one the torches started to flicker and go out. Josh got behind Suzy as she notched an arrow into her bow and pointed it at the farthest torch still lit.

As soon as it started to flicker, she released the arrow.

The torch went out and something screamed. It didn't sound like a human's scream. It was more animal. More primal.

She notched another arrow and pulled the bow tight.

Andre had drawn his sword and stood next to her. The only one looking behind them, in the direction they had originally been heading, was Josh.

In the faint flicker of the torch Suzy had just lit, he saw a familiar shape emerge from the darkness.

"Creeper!" he yelled and drew his sword. He dashed forward and swung at the Creeper, to knock it back before it exploded.

Instead of getting knocked back, the Creeper ducked away from the sword, and hissed loudly.

If it exploded now, all three of them would be caught in the blast. Notch had said they were stronger, but they could still be knocked out and killed in the program. They stood a better chance if he was the only one to get injured by the Creeper's explosive force.

He yelled as he charged forward with his head down and tackled the Creeper like a football player sacking a quarterback. He wrapped his arms around the Creeper and lifted it slightly, driving it backward as he ran. The Creeper was flashing faster now.

With his head pressed against the Creeper, hoping he could survive a direct explosion, he hugged it tightly as he ran. The only thing he felt when it exploded was his eardrums compressing painfully; and then nothing.

Chapter 7

"Nooooo!"

Andre screamed at the same moment the Creeper exploded. He and Suzy were thrown backward down the tunnel from the force of the concussive blast. All the torches went out at once.

His ears rang and light filled the tunnel around them as Suzy lit another torch. She stuck it on the wall and they both ran forward.

Suzy put up an arm and stopped Andre from going over the edge of the newly created cliff. She lit another torch and placed it on the wall. It lit a cavern that stretched out around the small tunnel. The tunnel they had been walking through wasn't carved out of the solid mountain. It had been built like a covered bridge in the middle of an open space that stretched off into the blackness. Far below them, they could make out the faint glow of lava, and far above them, they could see an occasional pinpoint of light from where the cavern's ceiling had fallen way and left an opening to the surface above.

Andre looked over the edge of the cliff. They were hanging in the middle of a massive cavern without support. There was no way to climb down and find Josh.

The exploding Creeper had destroyed a

large section of the tunnel-bridge. If Josh had survived the explosion, he would have fallen all the way down to where the lava flowed. For a normal avatar, that would be too far to fall without dying. Notch had increased their health, but was it enough to survive the direct explosion of a Creeper, and then fall all the way down to the bottom of the world?

He turned on Suzy. "I told you we should have figured out how to fly."

Suzy looked out over the edge to the rest of the tunnel on the other side of the chasm. "We need to go back."

Andre grabbed her shoulders and made her face him. "What about Josh?!"

She pushed away from him. "We don't have time to worry about Josh right now."

"What if he's still alive down there?"

"If he is, then we can figure out how to rescue him after we have eliminated the Creepers. If he isn't, he's sitting in my dad's office with Notch."

"You're still worried about this little quest? Are you forgetting why we came here in the first place? It will take all four of us to trigger the cube. The same cube that fell down there with my brother. Isn't that more important than you being a hero to these people?"

"Of course he is. But unless you can tell me how to get down there from here, the only thing we can do is go back out and find another way into the caves."

As she headed back up the tunnel toward the surface exit, Andre looked down into the massive chasm below.

"If you're still down there, Josh, hold on. I'm coming back for you."

Chapter 8

Josh coughed himself awake and opened his eyes. He was staring at a low ceiling carved out of rock. He tried to sit up, but found himself bound to a bed with thick ropes.

He pulled against the ropes. He was able to take more damage, but he wasn't stronger and the ropes held him tightly to the bed.

He felt a presence enter the room and looked around. A young woman walked over to him and sat down on the chair next to the bed. She reached into a bowl, removed a small towel, and wrung the excess water from it as she smiled at him. "How are you feeling?"

"Where am I?"

She wiped the moist towel across his forehead. "You are safe. Sven said it was lucky you landed in the underground lake, or you would never have survived such a fall."

He looked at the bindings that stretched tightly across his whole body. "Why am I tied down?"

"You broke a lot of bones. It will take months for them to heal, and in that time, you mustn't move or they will not heal straight."

He looked at her as she continued to brush cool water across his forehead. "Who are you?"

A voice from behind her cut off what she

was about to say. "Helina! Come here!"

She placed the towel back in the water and quickly left without saying another word. From his angle tied to the bed, Josh couldn't see the door, but he heard harsh whispering before a man walked into his field of view.

The man stopped next to his bed and stared down at him. "What were you doing in the caves?"

Josh tried to move, but the bindings bit into his skin. "Who are you?"

The man looked him over, biting at his lower lip before finally responding. "My name is Sven. Now tell me why were you in the caves?"

Josh remembered that name from the city they were helping. "Sven. Sven. Are you Sven the Elder?"

Sven's eyes squinted. "I am Sven the Younger. He is my father."

Chapter 9

Andre slammed a fist on the spacious desk of Basia, the mayor of Estermead. "How can we help you if you won't help us?!"

Basia folded her hands together and placed them calmly on the table. It was obvious she was doing her very best to restrain herself from yelling back. Instead, she spoke quietly, forcing them to strain to hear her. "You are outsiders, so I will permit you a certain level of leniency." She focused her gaze on Andre. "But one more outburst like that, and I will not only take you to see Sven the Elder, but I will leave you there to rot out the remainder of your days."

Suzy pulled Andre away from the desk as she smiled at the mayor.

"Madam Basia, please excuse my friend. His brother became lost in the caves, and we were told by Elbertina that Sven knows the layout of those caves better than anyone."

"Sven the Elder is not allowed visitors."

Suzy leaned on the edge of the desk. "Can you please make an exception in our case?"

"I'm sorry. There are no exceptions."

Andre approached the desk again, speaking calmly this time. "We have what it takes to end the Creeper threat. All we need is for Sven to tell us another way in to the caves."

"He does not have the information you seek."

"But Elbertina said..."

Basia cut him off. "Elbertina has led you astray. Sven the Elder does not know anything about the caves, the Creepers, or anything. He has been in that hospital since before I was born. Even if he did know something, it has been so long since he talked with another human being, he wouldn't be able to relate it to you, or anyone, in a way that could be understood."

Suzy's ear tickled and she scratched at it. It only did that when she thought of something important. "Is there anyone else we can talk to? What about his family?"

Basia shrugged. "His wife passed away several years ago. He did have a son, but he left the city when he was fifteen to make a new life elsewhere."

Suzy grabbed Andre and pulled him after her as she left the mayor's office. "Thank you for your help Madam Mayor."

Once they were outside the government building, Andre pulled free of Suzy's grasp. "Thank you for your help? She didn't help us."

Suzy smiled. "Remember when Elbertina was taking us around the city?"

Andre nodded so she continued. "She

pointed out a boarded up house and said it was the old house of Sven the Elder."

"So?"

"I noticed that some of the boards looked new as if they had been placed there recently."

"So?"

"So... somebody's been going into that house."

"And?"

"And they're looking for something."

"What could they be looking for in an abandoned house?"

"My guess is something of sentimental value."

"Who would be sentimental over anything

in that old house?"

Suzy smiled. "Since Sven the Elder is locked up in the hospital, my guess is, it's his son."

Chapter 10

After the sun went down, Suzy and Andre hunched in the bushes and waited. After a while, they could hear the explosions in the distance as the Creepers began their nightly attack.

Everyone old enough to fight was stationed along the inner wall on the other side of the city with bows and arrows, ready to repel the Creepers when they breached the hastily rebuilt outer wall. Everybody too young or too old to help was moved to the government building at the center of town.

Sven's abandoned house was close to the

outer wall, but on the other side of the city. With everyone else focused on fighting the Creepers, or huddling together in the center, the neighborhood around his house was deserted.

Deserted except for the two adventurers watching the house.

Andre parted the bushes slightly and peered out. "Are you sure someone is going to break into the house again tonight?"

Suzy sat next to him, holding her legs up to her chin tightly to fend off the chilly air. "Not just anyone."

"The mayor said he left and was never heard from again."

"If someone was going to break into an old house without wanting to return, they wouldn't take the time to repair the boards that sealed the house. They would break in and let the police scratch their heads as to who did it. Whoever they are, they don't want anyone to notice they have been going inside. The fact that the boards were put back the last time means that whoever was there did not find what they were looking for."

"You think he's coming back tonight?"

"I think he has been here every night for the past month."

"What makes you say that?"

"The Creepers."

"The Creepers?"

"They have been focusing their attack on the wall as far as possible from this house for the past month. It's the perfect plan to keep anyone from seeing him sneak in and then back out again."

"What? That only makes sense if he were..." Andre stopped talking and looked at her.

She blew into her hands to warm them against the cold and finished his sentence. "...controlling the Creepers."

He finally found his voice. "That's not possible. Creepers are monsters. Not pets."

"I'm not ignoring any possibilities. Who

knows what Herobrine has been doing for the last fifty years?"

"You think he's behind this?"

"I don't know, but..."

She stopped talking, put a finger to her lips, and pointed toward the house. Andre followed her gaze and saw a darkened figure in a hooded cloak dart from the shadows of a nearby house to the front of the abandoned house.

He glanced around and then motioned toward the house he had just left. A second cloaked figure ran across to meet him.

Once the second person joined him, he pulled on the planks nailed across the front door. They swung out like a door on a hinge, allowing them to both slip inside. As soon as the two figures disappeared through the door, the planks swung back again to rest against the door, looking like they were still nailed across the doorway.

"Clever," Suzy whispered as she started to get up.

Andre grabbed her arm. "What are you doing?"

"I'm going in to see what they're up to."

"There could be more waiting where we can't see them."

She scanned the darkness of the neighborhood around her. "I don't think so."

"There are still two of them."

"There are two of us. And we're tougher."

She pulled her arm out of Andre's grip and dashed across the street.

"Why did I have to get stuck in a Minecraft world with Joan of Arc?" he murmured to himself as he dashed across the street to catch up with her.

Chapter 11

Still bound tightly to the bed, Josh inhaled deeply, counted to ten, and then exhaled sharply. The ropes loosened briefly and he tugged his arm out from under them. Once his arm was free, the ropes loosened enough for him to wriggle out of the bed.

He stood up and flexed his back, his legs, and his arms. During the last couple of hours he had been tied to the bed, he had healed completely. And he felt even stronger than before.

Even though it had hurt more than he had ever imagined it would, he had survived the

Creeper detonation and the fall, although he didn't remember much after the explosion.

For the first time, he was able to look around the cave, and his eyes fell onto a steel door with a small barred window. He walked over to it, peered inside, and jumped back as a bearded face appeared at the little window. "Get me out of here!"

"Who are you?"

The man clung to the bars with dirty hands and nodded with his head. "The keys are over there."

Josh looked to where the man indicated and saw the key ring dangling from a hook. He looked back at the man. "Who are you?"

"My name is Mason. And we have to hurry if we want to get out of here before they come back."

Josh recognized his name. "Mason? Your sister thinks you're dead."

"Did she say that?"

"No, but it was more about what she didn't say."

"Well I'm not. Get me out of here."

Josh grabbed the keys and unlocked the door. Mason rushed out of the tiny cell, grabbed some torches from the table, and ran for the main door. "Let's go."

Josh paused at the door. "I can't. I have to destroy the spawner."

"The what?"

"It's the thing that generates Creepers."

Mason shook his head. "It won't do any good. He's training them. He's making them smarter. We have to stop him. Once we stop him, we can stop the Creepers."

"We can stop both of them if we stop the Creepers first. Do you know where the spawner is?"

"You mean the Creeper nest?"

"Yes, the nest."

"Yes."

"Will you take me there?"

"I can show you where it is, but you are on your own if you want to try to destroy it."

"Why won't you help me?"

"Because I know it won't do any good. There are other nests. The only way to stop all the Creepers is to stop Sven the Younger."

Chapter 12

Suzy snuck up to the front of the abandoned house. Andre was right behind her. "I don't like this Suzy. This is breaking and entering."

She pulled on the boards and they swung open easily.

She smiled at Andre. "It's not breaking and entering if it's unlocked. Besides, this is Minecraft, not the real world."

He shook his head. "Everyone else here doesn't know that."

She slipped inside and looked back at Andre. "Are you coming?"

He looked around and finally followed her into the house.

He let the door swing back on its own, and it slammed shut with a loud smack. They both cringed and froze.

"Do you think they heard that?" Andre whispered.

"I hope not," she whispered back.

They stood perfectly still; listening for any indication that someone was coming to investigate the noise. When no one came, they crept forward through the dark house down a long hallway with rooms on either side. Suzy heard a noise from deeper inside the house. She stopped moving forward and put a hand up. Andre was looking behind him as he crept behind her and didn't see that she had stopped. He ran into her and she lost her footing. Falling forward, she let out a small cry as her knee landed on something hard and sharp.

She clamped her own hand around her mouth and listened.

The sounds she had heard stopped.

From up ahead, she heard the creak of a stair.

She backpedaled, pushing Andre back with her. "What's going..."

She clamped a hand around his mouth and pushed him into a small room off to one side of the hallway. She kept pushing until they were inside a small closet. She leaned forward and pulled the closet door closed just as a lamp lit up the hallway.

She crouched next to Andre and put her finger to her mouth with one hand while pointing at the closet door with the other.

He nodded and stayed quiet.

Peeking through the wood slats of the closet door, she watched the light increase until both figures were standing in the doorway of the room she and Andre were hiding in.

The first figure pulled the cloak from his head. "What is it?"

The second figure pulled his cloak back. Only, it wasn't a he; it was a she. She held the lamp high and looked into the room. "I thought I heard something."

Suzy sat back away from the closet door. She didn't want the light to reflect off her face should either of them look her way.

The woman lowered the lamp. "I guess it's nothing."

The man headed back down the hallway. "Come on. Only a couple more days and we will be there."

The light receded until darkness filled the hallway. Only then did Suzy let out the breath she had been holding. "That was close."

"Too close," Andre said. "Let's get out of here before they catch us."

Suzy shook her head. "I want to see what they are up to."

"They almost caught us. I don't think we should press our luck."

Suzy opened the closet door. "They said they were almost there. Where is there?"

"I don't know, and I don't care. I say we get out of here."

"You can leave if you want to. I'm following them."

Andre let out a big sigh and followed Suzy down the hallway.

She stopped at the door that led to the

underground cellar and listened. "It sounds like they are digging."

Andre shrugged. "This is Minecraft. Digging is what it's all about."

Suzy opened the door slowly, the hinges creaking. She stopped when the sounds below stopped. She waited silently until the digging sounds resumed. She pushed the door open just enough to get through and stepped onto the stairs. The wooden step let out the biggest creak as her weight pressed down on it. The digging sounds stopped again and the light increased quickly from the cellar below as someone raced to the bottom of the stairs.

Chapter 13

Josh and Mason peeked around the corner. Two Creepers stood guard in front of an iron door. They leaned back out of sight.

Mason quietly slid his bow from over his head. "If you want to destroy the Creeper's nest, it is right behind that door."

"How do you know?" Josh asked.

"Sven showed it to me as proof that there was nobody who could stop him."

"Why is he doing this?"

"I guess he is taking revenge on the city. He blames them for his dad going crazy."

"Did he try to talk to anyone in the

government about his dad?"

"I don't think so. I didn't even know he was alive until he captured me."

"Why did he show you everything?"

"I think he's proud of what he's doing and what he's accomplished with the Creepers."

"So how do we get in there and stop him?"

"Like this."

Mason notched an arrow and pulled back hard. He swung around the corner and let go. The arrow whistled through the air and connected with the first Creeper. At that same moment, he let fly the second arrow.

Both Creepers fell over; dead.

Mason strode up to the iron door and spun

open the lock. He pushed the door open and waved Josh inside. "You wanted to destroy the Creeper's nest, here you go. I'm going after Sven."

Josh grabbed Mason's arm as he turned to leave. "Stay and help me destroy the nest and I will help you get Sven."

Mason shook his head. "Sven left. That means it is night and the Creepers are attacking my city right now. I can return with an army come daylight and destroy the whole cave system if I have to, but right now, my sister needs me."

Mason ran off and disappeared around the corner.

Josh turned back around and stepped through the iron door.

Once inside, he heard a faint click and looked down. He had triggered a floor switch. Bright lights ignited one after another along the ceiling of a massive cavern. Josh stepped forward to the railing of the balcony he was on and looked down at the floor of the cavern. Thousands of Creepers stood in row after row; lined up like they were preparing for a parade; or an invasion.

As soon as all the lights were on, the Creepers all turned their heads as one, and looked up at Josh.

Chapter 14

Just as the man and woman reached the bottom of the stairs, Suzy backed away from the door and tripped over Andre who had been too close behind her.

They landed in a heap just as the man reached the top of the stairs and grabbed Andre and Suzy in his strong hands.

He lifted them off the ground and spun them around to face him. "What have we here?"

Andre hung limply in his hands, willing to accept his fate, while Suzy struggled against his iron grip. "Let me go!"

The man tossed her down. She landed at the woman's feet and was grabbed and held immediately.

The man set Andre down slowly and bent down to look him directly in the eyes. "How did you get here?"

Suzy pulled, but the woman held on to her tightly. "We know you are controlling the Creepers."

He pulled Andre with him as he approached Suzy. "What makes you think I'm controlling the Creepers?"

"When Elbertina told me the story of how you left as a little boy, and pointed out this house, I saw that the boards around the door were newer than the rest around the windows. It made sense that you would return to your childhood home, using the Creeper attacks to hide the fact you were sneaking into the city. What I don't know is why?"

Sven leaned forward. "You want to know why?"

Suzy met his stare with one of her own. "Yes."

He smiled. "Then I'll show you. No, wait. I'll do better than show you."

Sven handed Andre over to the woman. "Helina. You take the docile one. I can handle the spirited one."

He grabbed Suzy by the collar and pushed

her in front of him as they headed down the

stairs and into the underground cellar.

Chapter 15

Josh stared down at the army of Creepers, who were all staring back up at him like they were waiting for him to do something.

But what were they waiting for?

He decided not to find out.

As he turned, he saw the outline of a small cage with the spinning form of a Creeper inside.

The spawner!

Only, it was in the middle of the Creeper army.

He had survived the blast of one Creeper and lived; but Notch had mentioned that they weren't immortal. There was no way he would survive the blast of a thousand Creepers.

He looked down at them. None of them had moved, even though they all seemed to know he was on the balcony. Maybe they were frozen in place and he could get to the spawner to destroy it without any of them coming after him.

He walked along the edge of the platform, every Creeper watching him intently. It was driving him crazy. What were they waiting for?!

He stopped at the top of the ladder that would take him down to the ground level, where a thousand Creepers waited patiently.

Right about now he wished he had listened to Andre and taken the time to figure out how to fly.

He took three deep breaths and gripped the handles of the ladder. He swung himself around and started his descent, the Creepers watching his every move.

He stopped a few feet from the ground and twisted around to look at the closest row of Creepers. They hadn't moved, but they were all watching him closely. He had never been more creeped out in his life. For the first time, he understood where they got their name.

He was only a few feet away from the first row, but they hadn't moved, or hissed, or flashed, or exploded. He was well within their range to go after him. But they weren't doing anything but watching.

He set one foot on the floor and looked at the Creepers.

They stayed right where they were.

He set the other foot on the ground and spun around to face them.

They stayed still, but every head was turned in his direction.

He took a couple steps in one direction and stopped.

The only reaction from the Creepers was the slight movement of their heads as they tracked him.

He stood up straight and took a step toward one of the Creepers. It didn't do anything but watch him. He walked all the way up to it and put a hand out to touch it. He jumped back as the Creeper purred like a kitten.

What?!

He reached out again to pet the Creeper. It nuzzled into his hand and purred louder. He pet the one next to it. It also purred and moved closer to him.

He moved forward, the Creepers letting him walk into their ranks. He walked right up to the spawner without a single Creeper hissing at him or threatening to explode.

Maybe these were different types of Creepers. Not ones designed for warfare or blowing up.

It didn't matter. He had to destroy the spawner if he wanted to prevent Sven from making more of them.

He drew out his sword as quietly as he could and raised it over his head, ready to bring it down on the spawner and destroy it.

The Creeper closest to him hissed. He looked over at it, and watched as its eyes turned red. Not completely red, but a flickering orangey-red, like the inside of the eyes were made of fire.

More hissing began all around him. As he looked, more and more of the Creeper's eyes ignited with an internal flame. He raised the sword higher, and the hissing increased.

Somehow, they knew exactly what he was about to do.

And they didn't like it.

Chapter 16

Andre's hands were starting to blister as he swung the pickaxe against the rock, a tiny piece breaking off and falling to join the rest of the tiny pieces of rock at his feet. He looked over at Suzy who was swinging her pickaxe against the solid rock, a small pile of rock pieces lying at her feet as well. "Let's help these people, she said. Let's be heroes, she said."

She gave him a stern look. "I never said that."

He swung again, his pickaxe sticking into the rock. "Look at us now. We're helping the bad guy. We're not heroes. We're henchmen!"

Sven called over from where he was reclining comfortably in a chair, eating a mince pie. "More digging, less talking."

Andre quietly mimicked Sven in a mocking tone. "More digging, less talking."

Sven leaned forward. "What?!"

Andre looked at him. "Nothing." He pulled his pickaxe out of the rock and resumed digging.

After a few more chunks of rock fell at his feet, he stopped and turned to Sven. "Just what are we looking for?"

Sven glared at him. "Keep digging."

Andre dropped his pickaxe on the ground.

"No more digging until you tell me why we are doing this."

Sven leapt from the chair, grabbed Andre by the collar, lifted him up, and slammed him against the stone wall. "Do not challenge me boy!"

Andre hung limply in the man's arms. "I'm not challenging anyone. I just want to know why I'm doing this."

Sven got close to his face. He met Sven's stare with one of his own. Sven finally let him go. He dropped to the ground, but landed on his feet and stayed standing.

Sven spun around and walked back to his chair. As he sat down, he waved a hand around the tunnel. "Fine. We are currently under the hospital, where the people of this town have kept my father prisoner since I was a small boy."

Suzy rested against her pickaxe. "They told me your father went insane."

A vein pulsated on the side of Sven's neck. "He didn't go insane! That was a lie to cover up the truth! He only did what the mayor asked him to do. And for that, he was imprisoned for life."

Andre frowned. "I don't get it. Why would the mayor lock him up if he did what the mayor asked?"

"Because the mayor was afraid he would

talk about the Creeper project."

Suzy moved forward. "Your father was involved with the Creepers?"

"Involved? He created the Creepers."

Andre waved a hand dismissively. "Wait, wait, wait. Your dad made Creepers? Why would he do that?"

"My father was a young scientist, and when someone attacked the town, someone very powerful whose name I will not mention..."

Andre and Suzy looked at each other. They knew exactly who he was referring to.

Sven continued. "He nearly destroyed us, so the mayor hired my father to create monsters to defend our city. But when the first tests resulted in the destruction of a farmhouse, the people thought they were sent by Him. The mayor, wanting to keep the secret that he was behind the Creepers, locked up my father, burned all the records that pointed to the mayor's involvement, and buried the project."

Suzy nodded. "You have been sending Creepers to attack the city to provide cover for the nightly digging so you can break your father out of the hospital."

Sven smiled. "A brilliant plan, if I do say so myself."

Suzy took another step forward. "There's just one little flaw in your plan."

Sven frowned. "Oh, yeah? What's that?"

"Us!"

She swung the pickaxe at his head. Sven ducked and Andre tackled him to the ground. They struggled, each trying to gain the upper hand and win this wrestling match when a sudden crash from the other end of the tunnel made them all stop and look.

The ceiling had collapsed and a man with a long shaggy beard and white hair poked his head down through the hole. He dropped down and walked up to the three of them lying intertwined on the ground.

His forehead wrinkled as he looked at them.

And then his face lit up with recognition.

"Sven?"

Chapter 17

Josh lowered the sword slowly and tucked it back in his belt.

The Creepers stopped hissing and resumed their quiet purring.

These Creepers were not mindless, walking, blocks of dynamite. They understood what the spawner was. And they knew that without it, there would not be any more of them.

They were behaving like parents protecting their young.

One of the Creepers broke rank and stepped out of the line it was in. It approached Josh slowly. Josh stepped to the side and let the Creeper pass by him. It took a couple more steps, then stopped to turn and look at him. It looked at him briefly, then looked in the direction it was walking, and then back at him.

Was it trying to lead him somewhere?

The Creeper took another step and then looked back at him again.

"You want me to follow you?"

The Creeper continued walking and Josh followed.

The Creeper led him to a pedestal with a helmet sitting on it. The Creeper looked at the helmet, and then looked at Josh.

He pointed to the helmet. "You want me to

put that on?"

The Creeper took a step back.

Josh lifted the helmet up and placed it on his head.

He heard the Creeper hiss. A half-second later, the speaker in the helmet crackled to life and words came out, sounding like what he expected a snake to sound like if a snake could talk, with the "s" sounds extended longer than necessary.

"Lead usssss."

Chapter 18

Andre and Suzy sat on the floor of the cellar, tied together.

Sven and his father, Sven, were hugging for the hundredth time.

Sven the Younger was smiling so big, his face threatened to split in half. "I never thought I would see you again Father."

Sven the Elder smiled back. "Did you find my notebook? Are the Creepers ready?"

"Yes. And I followed your instructions exactly as you wrote them."

"Good boy. I knew I could count on you."

Andre struggled against the ropes that

bound him to Suzy, but they were too tight. He thought Notch had said they would be like superheroes in this world. He didn't feel like a super anything at the moment. He couldn't even break through simple woven ropes.

Sven the Younger pointed to the two kids. "What do we do with them?"

Sven the Elder looked at them. "Nothing. They will suffer with the rest of the city when we return with the Creepers."

A commanding voice called out from the base of the stairs. "Not so fast Svens!"

Everyone looked to see Mason pushing a terrified Helina in front of him, and gripping a sword. "I knew I would find you here."

Both Svens picked up swords and faced Mason.

"You can't take both of us by yourself, Mason." said Sven the Younger.

Mason smiled. "What makes you think I came alone?"

Just then, several soldiers rushed down the stairs and pointed their drawn bows at the two Svens.

Mason pushed Helina toward them. "It's over."

Sven the Elder puffed up his chest. "It's not over. I have an army of Creepers on their way to destroy the city."

Mason laughed. "Yeah, about that."

Chapter 19

Josh rode on the back of a Creeper, a thousand Creepers kicking up dust as they ran behind him. Using the translation helmet, he directed his army of Creepers to attack those still attacking the city.

Creepers exploded everywhere, the sound hundreds of times louder than the original attacks.

Within minutes, the only Creepers left were those under his command.

He stopped their forward movement and pulled the army of Creepers away from the city walls.

All along the edge of the wall, people began cheering.

News spread quickly that the Creeper threat was over.

The three heroes who had come to save their town had done it.

Chapter 20

Mayor Basia stood before the three heroes in her office.

"I would like to thank you for saving our city from Sven, again. It is true that my father, while he was mayor, commissioned Sven the Elder to build a Creeper army. But then Sven decided to use it to take control of the city and become the new mayor without holding any elections. He was going to hold the city hostage instead. He was deemed insane by a tribunal and placed in the hospital."

"Why didn't your father tell anyone the real reason?" Suzy asked.

"Those were troubling times and my father decided that the Creeper army was too dangerous, even for an elected mayor to control. So he buried the project in the caves where no one could get to it."

Andre nodded. "That is until Sven the Younger showed up and brought them all back."

Basia smiled. "If it weren't for the three of you, they would have succeeded in their plan and taken over the city. I can't imagine what would have happened then."

Josh smiled. "Then it's a good thing we happened by."

Basia sat down at her desk. "Are you sure I

can't convince you to stay a few days longer. The city has prepared a feast in your honor."

Suzy shook her head. "I wish we could, but we are on a quest to find the one known as Him."

Basia stiffened. "He is very dangerous. Why do you want to find Him?"

Andre stood up straighter. "We are going to take Him away from your lands and save everyone."

Basia's shoulders dropped in relief. "Oh good. Which way are you headed?"

Josh unfolded his map. "It looks like our next stop is a town called Silverrock."

Basia's face grew serious. "Be careful. That

town is in the heart of dragon territory."

Find out what happens to Josh and Andre.

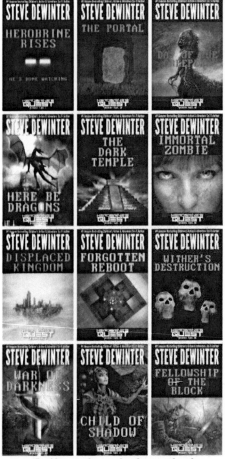

Collect the whole series!

Other Books by the Author

A is for Apprentice (Fantasy)

Oliver Twist: Victorian Vampire (Fantasy-Horror)

A Tale of Two Cities with Dragons (Fantasy)

Shade Infinity (Thriller)

Peacekeepers X-Alpha Series (Thriller)
    Inherit the Throne
    The Warrior's Code

Steampunk OZ Series (Science Fiction Novellas)
    Forgotten Girl
    The Legacy's World
    Emerald Shadow
    The Future's Destiny
    The Dangerous Captive
    Missing Legacy
    Shadow of History
    The Edge of the Hunter

Jason and the Chrononauts (Kid's Adventure Series)
    The Chronicle of Stone
    The Winter's Sun
    The Gateway's Mirror
    The Forgotten Oracle
    The Prophecy's Touch
    The Dawn Legend

Be the first to know about Steve DeWinter's next book. Follow the URL below to subscribe for free today!

http://bit.ly/BookReleaseBulletin

CPSIA information can be obtained at www.ICGtesting.com
Printed in the USA
LVOW07s1619230216

476355LV00007B/732/P